# 40 OUNCES OF

## *Tears*

# 40 OUNCES OF

## *Tears*

### DANIELLE CHERY

Charleston, SC

www.PalmettoPublishing.com

*40 Ounces of Tears*

Copyright © 2022 by Danielle Chery

All rights reserved

First Edition

Paperback ISBN: 978-1-63837-945-4
eBook ISBN: 978-1-63837-946-1

*For those who have been or continue to be,*
*severely affected by alcoholism. You're not alone.*

# CONTENTS

## chapter one

# THREE OUNCES

I sat alone on a lavender wool blanket in the middle of the living room floor playing with the toy piano given to me by my mother last Christmas. All the neighborhood parents banned their kids from coming over to our house. No one wanted to be around him and his cup, not even his own family.

I showed no indication to my mother that I was troubled by what happened to us last night. I had never seen her this broken before, and for some reason, there was no difference between her and the shattered pieces of window glass on the kitchen floor.

Most of Mr. Elmstruck's belongings were already outside on the grass. I watched her scurry back and forth from the bedroom to the living room to see if there was anything else left that had belonged to him. She gathered any items she could find, from books to broken sunglasses and even pictures that his face was already cut out of.

My mother knew that I was far more advanced than the average three-year-old. Everywhere she went, I was there, following her every step and keeping my eye on her each time she left my side. I could always feel her sadness, especially when she tried to hide it the most.

While she swept the cold wooden floor, a hard-sounding object rolled slowly from underneath the opposite side of the couch. A ray of sunlight shone directly from the living room window onto the object, catching my immediate attention. I'd seen this object before. Mr. Elmstruck used to play this weird game where he'd pretend like he wanted me to have it, and then as soon as I reached my hand out, he'd scream in my face, "Nope!"

I scooted toward the bottle, picking it up carefully so that it wouldn't fall out of my little hands. I was amazed by its odd shape and bubbly liquid. After a few minutes had passed, my quietness triggered suspicion in my mother.

"Electa, are you okay?" she asked in a hoarse tone.

When she didn't hear toys clashing together, she stopped sweeping and immediately walked over to check on her child attempting to drink a forty-ounce glass bottle. My small hands struggled to hold it firmly, but it didn't stop me from trying to put it up to my little lips.

"Electa!" she exclaimed, grabbing the glass bottle out of my hands.

"No, no, my sweet little angel. That's not for you to drink!"

Startled, I looked on sadly as she took it away from me and replaced it with a purple cup decorated with unicorns and gold stars. The bottle was still in her hand, and yet in that moment my little curious mind thought to drink the last few drops of fizzy liquid left in it. She inhaled and exhaled deeply.

"Enough is enough," said my mother as she shook her head, walking away in disbelief.

She tried to do everything she could to hold back her tears, but each time she swept up something broken, it reminded her that she was sweeping away broken pieces between her and Mr. Elmstruck. She didn't want to compete with his cup anymore. If there was any doubt in her mind, seeing me hold that forty-ounce bottle to my mouth was the last straw she needed to make sure that Mr. Elmstruck stayed out for good.

I continued to watch her. This time I didn't pretend not to. She walked over to the kitchen sink and poured out the remaining three ounces. She stared at the bottle with a disgusted look and placed it in the recycling bin, just like she did Mr. Elmstruck.

## chapter two

# EIGHT OUNCES

H e sat upright in his favorite mustard yellow recliner in front of the living room television, watching his favorite sports channel. He said very little when he didn't have his favorite cup in his hand. His bearded face and husky body sat erect as his piercing dark brown eyes followed each play.

Five years had passed since he moved back home to the only person who would tolerate every ounce of him: his mother. It wasn't often that I saw Ms. Elmstruck or spoke to her for that matter, but one thing I could say was that I couldn't wait to taste some of her baked lobster and parsley mac 'n' cheese, buttered biscuits, collard greens, and honey barbecue chicken. The scent of her Southern-style cooking filled the whole house as it traveled up to the third floor, where I was. She might not have cared about me much, but I could surely count on her to send me back home with a full belly, especially when Mr. Elmstruck was either passed out or nowhere to be found.

My mother let me visit Mr. Elmstruck every so often, mostly every other weekend, when she wasn't working the graveyard hours as a taxi cab driver. As I waited for supper, I played in Mr. Elmstruck's room, watching my favorite cartoon show,

*Gray Rugs.* He didn't like anyone touching his things, especially when he wasn't there.

After the game was over, Mr. Elmstruck invited one of his lady friends over. His mother wouldn't stop making up songs about demons being removed from every corner of her house. Somehow, she managed to get Mr. Elmstruck irritated enough where he left with his guest. I opened the door to make sure the coast was clear, slowly closing and locking it.

Although Mr. Elmstruck forbade me not to touch his things, I couldn't help but wonder what he was hiding. There was one particular draw that he only opened at night when he had his cup in his hand. Looking at the small wooden nightstand with an empty customized football coaster, I knew I didn't have much time. He was very organized, especially when it came to his keys, tools, and other items he had multiples of.

I found a little black box engraved with "6394" on his dresser that also had a customized code on it. I immediately began thinking of what the combination number could be until I heard the downstairs door open, followed by a ring. I quickly put the box back exactly where I found it and sat back on the bed as if I wasn't just attempting to creep through his personal belongings like the curious eight-year-old I was.

"Lec! Get downstairs!" yelled Ms. Elmstruck. "Come back down here and wash your hands for supper!"

"Yes, ma'am," I said, immediately running down the stairs.

Ms. Elmstruck was a short dark-brown-skinned woman with a singing voice similar to Aretha Franklin. She dressed as if she was going to church every day, but there weren't enough fine suits that could mask her sassy and snappy attitude.

I went to the living room and sat on the opposite recliner from Mr. Elmstruck's chair. My plate was on a black television tray table along with a glass of orange sunny delight, a napkin, and utensils.

I turned around to thank her but was afraid that saying something as simple as that would only interfere with her peeking through the kitchen window at Mr. Elmstruck and his lady friend. Ms. Elmstruck sneakily looked through the kitchen window, watching them laugh loudly and pass each other shots of vodka. I waited for her to walk back in the living room.

"Thank you for dinner. May I have more after this plate?" I asked bashfully.

Ms. Elmstruck did not respond right away but this time it wasn't because she wanted to purposefully ignore me. By the look of disgust on her face, I could tell she was upset at yet another strange streetwalker drunk outside on the porch with Mr. Elmstruck.

"No problem, child," she said in her deep Southern accent. "Who else gonna feed you when you're here?"

She walked back to the kitchen and continued to do the dishes while singing her gospel songs as if the sound of her voice was enough to trick the Lord into forgetting that she has a vile tongue. I was used to Ms. Elmstruck's complaints and comments about her son. As much as she despised him, she was all he had left.

Bathing times became my favorite after dinner when I went to Mr. Elmstruck's house. My mother would have thrown a fit if she knew that my bath time consisted of me rolling around in bubbles for an hour. I jumped and swam happily left and right until the water didn't have that fizzy look anymore.

As I was preparing to pull the drain and let the water out, I began hearing loud banging noises from downstairs as if something was hitting the walls. Mr. Elmstruck and his lady friend were stumbling in the house, bumping into things each step they took.

"Get yo raggedy butt over here, hooker!" he blurted. The woman was tall and skinny with a mocha brown complexion. She had short, black hair with bright purple highlights at the tips. She sat at the kitchen table and lit her cigarette with no regard to anyone but herself.

Ms. Elmstruck continued to clean and ignore the woman's existence. She went as far as sweeping the trash on her shoes in hopes that the woman would get up and leave. Rolling her eyes, the woman continued to pay no mind to Mr. Elmstruck's demands or his mother's attitude for that matter. She slowly took a drag of her cigarette and blew the remaining smoke in Ms. Elmstruck's face.

Mr. Elmstruck continued to charge up the staircase as the woman began to laugh hysterically as if falling on every step over and over was something to laugh about.

"Where are you going, fool?" she yelled. "If you take too long, I'm leaving, and you ain't getting nothing!" Ms. Elmstruck's eyebrows rose right on time like sunrise.

"He's better off getting nothing from you, if he hasn't already," she muttered.

"Get the hell up out of here then! I...I...don't need you. And leave my goddamn taste on the table before you leave!" yelled Mr. Elmstruck in a slurred tone.

The woman shook her head and continued to finish the last few drops of liquor in her cup. Mr. Elmstruck's head was spinning as the liquor began to spill all over his hand. I could hear him stumbling up the stairs to the third floor, where I was. He barged through the bathroom door, making it slam against the wall. I curled up in a little ball in the tub, afraid of what he was going to do next. He didn't bother to lift the toilet seat up and began peeing all over the place, still drinking the cup in his hand.

I tried not to move, but it was no use. He blinked several times and began staring at me without saying a word. As he slowly walked towards the tub, his eyes started spiraling in different directions as if he were possessed. Mr. Elmstruck could barely walk. He paused with each step he took, growing in rage from the liquid spilling onto his hand. Each drop that didn't make it to his tongue irritated him even more.

"H-H-Hey, sweety, what's the matter? Are you okay?" said Mr. Elmstruck as he suddenly stopped swaying from side to side and stood still in front of the tub like a statue. His breath had a foul scent of cigarettes and old contaminated sewage water. Both my arms were wrapped around my legs tightly. The closer he came, the tighter I squeezed my legs together.

"Let me get a kiss! Now!" He yelled.

As he leaned forward to kiss me, I slowly turned my face away while still trying to cover my developing body from his eyes. His pants were still unbuttoned and barely clinging onto his hips. I could tell he was blind to my innocence. His awareness faded in and out as he began swaying side to side again. At that moment, he did not know the difference between a streetwalker and an innocent eight-year-old girl, even if they both looked him right in the eyes.

"You're scaring me!" I exclaimed.

A warm tear instantly rolled down my right cheek. He grunted and took a step back, looking at himself in the bathroom mirror. I could tell that whatever was left of his consciousness screamed for him to walk away and leave me be. He struggled to keep his balance. His pants were still unbuttoned, exposing his manhood right in front of me. I closed my eyes and pretended not to notice once he directed his attention to me again.

"Sweetheart, I'm...I'm, you know, what, dammit! forget this." Mr. Elmstruck turned around abruptly and tripped over the bathroom trash, stumbling right in front of the toilet. He hit his head against the wall and didn't make a sound. I quickly pulled the bathtub plug, letting the water escape. As Mr. Elmstruck lay on the floor breathing heavily, I grabbed my towel and ran to Ms. Elmstruck's bedroom, locking the door behind me. He didn't notice me leaving, and part of me didn't want him to either.

The next morning, I woke up to the sound of thunder and downpour. Ms. Elmstruck was already downstairs making Sunday breakfast. The smell of her grits, scrambled eggs, sausages, and buttery toast drove me out of bed. I went to Mr. Elmstruck's room, where my things were. The door was cracked open. I began packing my things so that once my mother picks me up, she doesn't have to look at Mr. Elmstruck or his mother longer than she needed to.

When I went to grab my gold bracelet from the dresser, I noticed that the drawer that had the little black box engraved with "6394" was open. I hesitated to touch it again because it wasn't like him to leave it exposed so carelessly for anyone else to see. I slowly lifted the top of the box and discovered a small picture of my mom when she was in high school. I looked underneath it and saw two of the same photos of all three of us with the writings on the back—"Forever my lavender loves 6.3.94." The last picture was a photo of him holding my long-lost brother Samion. I continued to sort through the contents of the box and stumbled upon a picture of Mr. Elmstruck and Samion's mother. I noticed that the majority of the right side of the photo had been burned.

There was a knock on the door. It was Ms. Elmstruck.

"Lec, I'm going to rest. Your breakfast is on the table downstairs. Make sure you go eat. You hear?"

"Yes, ma'am," I said in a trembling voice. "I'll be right down."

"And, Lec, make sure to keep the door open at all times. He doesn't pay any rent here. I always want my doors open and to know what's going on. Understand?"

"Yes, ma'am. I understand."

She walked away while looking suspiciously around. She could never stop snooping when Mr. Elmstruck was around. The hole in the bathroom wall made her even more paranoid of being in the house with him.

My heart was racing as I took my bag and ran downstairs. Mr. Elmstruck listened to a lot of different music, especially jazz. I could hear the loud music playing while Ms. Elmstruck mumbled curse words under her breath. Needless to say, she was not at all happy about the noise.

He sat quietly in his yellow recliner with his eyes closed, moving his right index finger from left to right as if he was leading an orchestra band. I quietly walked into the living room and sat on the couch.

"You slept well last night?" he asked in his deep, militant voice.

"Yes, sir," I responded, still puzzled and uncomfortable from what happened last night.

"Uh…can I ask you a question? Are you feeling better? I mean, are you okay from last night?" I asked.

"Of course, I'm okay, never been better. Why?" Asked Mr. Elmstruck.

From his defensiveness, I could tell either he had no idea what I was talking about or he chose not to remember. Either way, he genuinely looked like he had no idea what happened last night. If he didn't remember, maybe the bluish green bruise on his head would help remind him.

"No reason," I said. "Just asking because you have a lump on your head from last night."

"Oh! I don't even know how it got there, but I'll be fine. Finish eating so we can head on out to the park before your mother comes. The sun is back out, and I need to go pick up something."

Shortly after breakfast, we departed to a nearby park in the neighborhood. I loved when Mr. Elmstruck put me on his shoulders during our walks to the park, except for when we'd see women on the way who'd flirt with their eyes while complimenting how cute my hair or outfit was. Most times he would exchange numbers with them and bring me back to his house.

When we went to the park, I saw some kids I knew who lived around Mr. Elmstruck's neighborhood. One of those kids was my best friend, Amidah. She recently moved with her mom across the way, and it was my first time seeing her since school ended. While we were laughing and playing jump rope, an odd, strange man walked in, stumbling through the park gates.

"Check out the goofy-looking guy!" joked Carl, one of the neighborhood boys. "He reminds me of my uncle Doobie. He always has that stupid red cup in his hand."

"I heard that guy always comes out at night into the park and scares kids," said Amidah.

"Well, why is he here so early then?" I asked.

The bald-headed man had on black sunglasses, baggy jeans, and a long black shirt with the word "Renaissance" in red font. A couple of his front teeth were missing from the top and bottom, but it didn't stop him from smiling.

"What's up, dog! My man, I ain't seen ya in a while. Where you've been hiding?" the man shouted as he ran to give Mr. Elmstruck a handshake.

"You know, man, just taking care of my mom, and I got the little one here, so just been handling my business, you know," said Mr. Elmstruck.

The bald man seemed confused as he put back his sunglasses and looked over at us. Carl began sticking out his tongue.

"Damn, one of those badass kids yours?" he asked as he put his glasses back on and burst into laughter and tears.

"Well, check this big wave right here, brother. This ain't no regular. This is the drink I was telling you about that hit you so hard you'll feel like you went underground!"

Mr. Elmstruck's eyes lit up. He quickly grabbed the bag from the odd man, thinking we all didn't notice, but we did.

"Thank you, brother. I got a little fine thang coming to-morrow. Let's see if that jam can take me to the mooooon!" he said jokingly.

The odd man stopped laughing and got serious for a moment.

"Well, be easy there, boy. My old girl added a special little ingredient. If you kill it too fast all at once, you might mess around and stay on the moon. You feel me?" whispered the man.

"I'm Mr. Elmstruck, boy! Nothing and no one could take me down. Don't let me remind you of who I am," he said.

Both men laughed as they nudged each other back and forth like two teenage boys.

"I'm out of here," said Carl in an irritated voice. "Not watching these two lovebirds any longer. Besides, I have to go meet my big brother and head home before the streetlights come on."

The black bag the man gave Mr. Elmstruck had a long brown paper bag with a large glass bottle in it. I watched him from the monkey bars pull it out to admire the written gold words that read, "40 oz. Bananas Premium."

He began taking large gulps simultaneously. This bottle wasn't like any other one I'd seen him with before. I continued to play hide-and-seek with my friend Amidah until the sun set, and it was time for her to go home.

"Amidah! Streetlights are on now!" yelled her mother from a window across the park.

"I have to go, Lec. Will I see you next weekend?"

"Not sure," I replied sadly. "It depends on how my momma feels. Lately he's been arguing with her a lot when he has his cup, and she said one day she's going to do something about it."

"I don't see you putting the gas to your feet, little girl!" yelled Amidah's mother.

"I gotta go. I'll talk to you soon." Amidah grabbed my arm and gave me a tight hug as if it was our last time we'd see each other.

I ran back to the bench where Mr. Elmstruck and the strange man were sitting. He was nowhere to be found. The only thing left was the brown paper bag and me. As I sat on the ground sobbing, I saw a vehicle pull up. I immediately got up and began to walk in the opposite direction. My heart was racing as I turned around and saw the door fly open.

"Electa! Oh, my goodness! I'm so glad you're alive!"

It was my mother. She ran and held me in her arms as I continued to sob like a baby.

"Don't cry. I'm here now. I'd rather be dead before I let him do this to you again," she said in a hoarse voice as tears began flowing down both her cheeks. We walked to the car and went straight home without getting my things from Mr. Elmstruck's house.

During the middle of the night, my mother and I woke up to banging noises on the front door. Mr. Elmstruck came to our house with a bat. He must've gone back to the park because he still had the brown paper bag in his hand that the odd man gave him. I sat quietly on my bedroom floor with the door cracked open, hoping that he wouldn't bust the windows again like he did last time when my mom kicked him out for good.

"How dare you leave our eight-year-old in the street just so you can go drink your life away!" yelled my mother as she stood in the doorway, refusing to let Mr. Elmstruck in our house.

"I didn't leave that little girl," said Mr. Elmstruck. "She was over there with the kids, and I told her I'll be right back." Mr. Elmstruck suddenly pushed the door open, prompting my mother to run into the kitchen and grab a knife from the drawer.

"Don't you ever leave my baby again. And since you want to go back to the army so bad, maybe you should. It's the only time you have your head out of the clouds."

"Fine!" shouted Mr. Elmstruck. "The army loves me more than you ever did anyway. I may not do shit for my daughter, but she will always be a loving child. Better be lucky I gave you something to love, stupid."

Mr. Elmstruck picked up his bat off the floor and walked towards my bedroom. I quickly turned off my night-light and went back under the covers. The door opened slowly, and I could hear him stumbling toward me. I squeezed my eyes tight shut and remembered that my mother wasn't too far. He kissed me on my forehead, and I could smell the foul scent of liquor and cigarettes on his breath.

Mr. Elmstruck left and did not return back to our house. My mother slept in the middle of the main hallway floor to make sure that he didn't. I lay asleep most of the night in my bed wondering if I'd ever see him again.

The next morning the phone rang, and it was Mr. Elmstruck's sister, Arlena. She and my mother were very close, and she often would help out with me, especially when my mother needed to work. She was the only one out of Mr. Elmstruck's family who treated my mother with respect and kindness.

"I am so sorry you had to deal with that knucklehead's bull," said Aunt Arlena. "He already took off to the military. He doesn't even know when he'll be back."

"He's better off there, Arlena. Hell would freeze over before I'd ever want to see him again," said my mother.

## chapter three

# SIXTEEN OUNCES

*ing, ring, ring!* The alarm clock went off at 7:00 a.m. After the fourth snooze, I figured I'd better get up before my mom became an alarm that I couldn't hit the snooze button on. Today was the day we began moving into our first house. Between preparing for my sweet sixteen birthday celebration and helping my mom prepare to move, it was hard to catch up on some sleep.

"Electa! Are you up? I need to stop at the house after the movers get here. I also have a meeting with the realtor at 8:30 a.m. to finalize a few things. Oh!"

"And our meeting with the decorator is at 9:30 a.m. We can't be late," I said at the same time as her.

"I know, Mom. I'm getting ready now. But can't I just have five more minutes?"

She held all one hundred birthday invitations over my trash can. "Now, Electa, or you could just forget about your party."

"Say no more, mama bear! I'm up!" I said sarcastically.

My mother knew how important this birthday party was to me. It wasn't just that it was a sweet sixteen that every teenager rave about. It was the first birthday celebration I had since I was eight, which I spent with Mr. Elmstruck.

I remembered it like it was yesterday, and I'd never forget it. At Ms. Elmstruck's request, Mr. Elmstruck and I had walked over to a nearby hair salon. She had believed my hair had not been done even though my mom had done it that morning for my birthday. He had gone out and had not returned until the hair store closed. When he had arrived, he banged on the door, and before the stylist addressed him, he had immediately ran up to me with a cake, tripping over a hair dryer cord and vomiting all over my hair and clothes. My mother was furious when she picked me up that night. I reeked of rotten eggs, cigarettes, and hot pork intestines. It didn't look as disgusting as it smelled.

All our things were already packed. We moved a few times over the years, so we were happy to finally settle in our new home right before I went off to college. The doorbell rang, and the movers arrived. There were four men, one of which looked familiar.

"Okay, fellas, we only have a couple fragile boxes to your right. Please be gentle with them," said my mother.

Time is money, and the men didn't waste any time to start loading our moving truck. I sat in the passenger seat after the movers finished loading all the heavy boxes that needed to go to the new house. I couldn't help but watch one of the movers. "Where do I know him from?" I asked myself. He had on a hat from the moving company and was in full uniform from top to bottom. I could tell he lost a little weight, but I couldn't quite put my finger on who he was. Before my mother got back into the truck, I quickly wrote down the number and address of the Strucker's Moving Company.

I could see the joy on my mother's face when we arrived at our new house. The exterior was painted lavender with white trim. My mother didn't waste any time starting to unpack. The decorator was already on her way. While she prepared to meet with her, I quickly ran upstairs to figure out where my room was and to call my partner in crime, Amidah. I noticed a room door down the hallway that was already halfway open. As I continued to walk, I could smell my mother's rosewater-scented perfume. She was already there.

When I pushed the door open, I saw that the room had nothing in it except a lavender wool blanket in the middle of a white carpeted floor. It was my mother's way of letting me know it was where she wanted me to be. As soon as I took out my phone, it began to ring. It was Amidah.

"Midah, girl, you need to come here and help me unpack and decorate this!" I said excitedly. "I need your touch of sweetness. It's so spacious, and I love the white carpeting!"

"Duh, Lec! Ain't no sweetness touch like the one I got!" she said jokingly. "Do you have a walk-in closet? Wait, if you're home right now I can come so that we can finalize the details for your sweet sixteen."

At that moment I paused. "I am, but when you get here, we need to talk. I need you to go somewhere with me. Do you have your car?" I asked.

I knew Amidah noticed a change in my tone. But if there was anyone who I'd need to ride with me on anything, it would be her.

"Lec, what crazy thing do you need to get us into now? You know what, details when I get there."

We spent most of the day unpacking and decorating our new home. While my mother was downstairs finalizing payment and contracts with the decorator, Amidah and I finalized the guest list. After weeks of planning, everything was finally done. We both lay down on the soft white carpet from exhaustion.

"Amidah, after dinner, I need you to drive to the Strucker's Moving Company. There's something I need to check out."

Amidah sighed heavily. "Okay, Lec, but if anything goes down, you owe me. I just got this car for one. And two—" Before I let Amidah finish her sentence, I hugged her.

"Thank you! I promise it isn't anything that would have us running from bullets."

We both laughed at the inside joke. Shortly thereafter my mother came to let us know that she was stepping out to get a few last-minute household items.

"Mom, I'll be back. We're just going to get a few things for my room too, then make a stop at Amidah's house."

"Electa…," my mom said suspiciously. "We don't have to do everything all at once today. And I thought you'd spend more time helping me get things situated in the house."

"I am, Mom. I'll be right back, okay?"

I kissed my mother, and we left to go to one of the locations of the Strucker's Moving Company.

"I'll explain in the car," I whispered to Amidah.

On our way to the Strucker's Moving Company, we stopped at a decor room store and picked up a few items for my room. The last thing I needed was for my mother to catch me in a lie by showing up empty-handed. We grew closer over the years without Mr. Elmstruck. I hadn't seen him since the day he left me at the park but for some reason, the older I got, the more I felt like I needed him. My mother and I talked about everything, but this thing I just couldn't talk to her about. There was something I'd been wanting to do for years, and that man from the moving company was the key to help me do it. My mother wouldn't understand; nobody would.

We arrived at an old fountain stone gray building that looked like it was going to collapse any minute. The words "Strucker's Moving Company" were written on the left side of the building in big red script font. I saw the same man who was part of the moving crew my mother hired. He was standing outside smoking a cigarette. Amidah parked the car not too far from where the entrance was. I could tell she wasn't making any more moves until I explained what we were doing here and why.

I put my right hand on her shoulder. "Amidah, please don't be mad at me."

"What do you expect, Electa? I'm always there for you when you need me. Lately you've been on detective mode, and all I ask is to know what's going on."

"You're right. I didn't want to tell anyone. Not even my best friend. The last few years, my mother has been working and saving to get the house. The last time we moved, I found her black address book with Ms. Elmstruck's number. And—"

Before I could finish my sentence, Amidah snapped her neck so fast I thought she broke it.

"Wait. This is about the Elmstrucks, Electa? You vowed to never speak or deal with them again, especially after what you found out about your brother, and what would your mom think?"

"I didn't ask you to judge me! I asked you to be a friend and just listen!" I shouted.

Amidah had a puzzled look on her face. She didn't say a word. I exited the car, slamming the door behind me. We were parked at the end of the corner out of sight, where no one could see us.

"Lec, just be careful. Whatever it is that you're doing, just call me if you need me to pull up in the front."

I began walking. I paid Amidah no mind. No one knew how it felt to have an empty hole for years that you couldn't fill. It only grew bigger with time. This was my only chance to find him.

The man turned around on his phone when I approached him. Startled, he turned around and quickly put his phone in his pocket.

"Oh shit! I thought you were my boss. My break was over an hour ago! Don't run up on me like that, lil girl. And who are you anyway? I don't got no money for Girl Scouts or your mama if you mine."

The man began laughing and coughing at the same time. I could tell that he had missing teeth on his top and bottom gums.

"You may not remember me, sir, but you know my father. I haven't seen him in many years and was wondering if you have a number I could call or know where I can find him."

He paused, gaping with his mouth open. The cigarette fell out as he took off his hat and scratched his bald head in confusion. I tried not to look at his mouth as he stared idly at me like a deer in the middle of a road watching an oncoming car.

"E-Erica, right? Wow! Your old man has been looking for you. You the same little rascal I saw at the park? Damn, you sure ain't little no more."

Trying not to burst into tears, I nodded, hoping he had some information that he could give me. He took out a pen full of lint from his stained uniform pants along with an old receipt that read "Triton Liquors." As he was writing Mr. Elmstruck's number and address down, I could see Amidah slowly driving up toward the entrance.

"What's your name?" I asked.

"You are asking a lot of questions, Erica. I'm not trying to go to jail. Shoot, standing here next to your little behind could get me arrested any second." He said jokingly.

"It's…Electa. And I wanted to just say thank you."

"You don't need a name for that, sweetheart," he said. "Name's Bron, but your old man and all folks back around the way know me as Bubb."

He handed me the paper, and it felt like fireworks had exploded inside me. I walked back over to the car where Amidah was, and we drove back to my house. The car ride was silent, but I could tell from the corner of my eye that she was happy to see me smile.

Amidah stayed over for dinner and helped my mother and I clean up and decorate the living room. After a long day of work, I couldn't wait to shower and call the number. After all, I wasn't sure I trusted this Bubb guy, but at least I had a place to start.

"Lec, I'm getting ready to go. Need anything else before I leave?"

"The bald-headed man from the park. He's my way of connecting back with the Elmstrucks, Amidah."

"Whoa! The creepy one with missing teeth," she said surprisingly. "How could I forget? He would always come out at night in the park to scare us and all the other neighborhood kids for fun. How do you know he's legit, Lec?"

I sat on my bed with the receipt in my hand. "I don't. But I trust it. I've waited all these years to see him again. I used to call his old number and hang up just to hear his voice. Your dad is great and all, but he's your dad."

Amidah walked over and sat right next to me. She held me, and I could tell she was worried. "I just don't want to see you get hurt, but I know how important it is for you to build that for yourself. I'm here whichever way it goes." When Amidah left, I went in the shower. As eager I was, I decided not to call. After all, I didn't know what I'd say.

The next few weeks were busy. My mother and I managed to get mostly everything unpacked and some decorating done in the house. I was so excited for my birthday celebration next weekend. I tried calling Mr. Elmstruck a couple of times, but for some reason there was no answer, and I didn't care to leave a voice mail. I was starting to think this Bubba guy played me for a fool.

Since my mother was having a few friends over for her monthly paint and sip night, I figured this would be the perfect Friday night to call Mr. Elmstruck one more time. The phone rang repeatedly but no answer. *Who am I kidding?* I thought. Suddenly my cell phone began ringing, and it was him.

"Hello, Mr. Elmstruck," I said nervously.

"Yes, this is he. Who am I speaking with?" he asked in his deep, militant voice.

"It's…It's…me, Electa," I said with an anxious tone.

"Lec! My baby, how are you? Gosh, I missed you so much! My boy over there at the moving company said he saw you, but I ain't believe him. I always prayed that you'd look for your father. You only have one."

I could hear how hoarse his voice was and some sniffles he made as he paused in midsentence to catch his breath.

"It's been, what, eight years since I last saw you. How's your mother doing?"

I couldn't find the words to say. Hearing his voice and hearing how much he never gave up on me filled a void that I was waiting for him to do for so long. "She's good. We just moved into our new house. She's a homeowner now like she's always wanted to be."

"Look at that! I always knew your mama would get a house. We always talked about it. Matter of fact, we were supposed to buy one right before she kicked my ass out. Man! I can't believe it's you, Lec. Your birthday is coming up next weekend. Can I see you?" he asked with a high-pitched voice.

"Umm, my mom is throwing me a birthday party, but I can see you this weekend. I don't have a car, but my friend Amidah can bring me. Bubba gave me the address. May I come tomorrow if you're free?" I asked.

"Yup!" he replied quickly. I heard voices in the background. "All right, see you tomorrow, Lec, yup. All right, have a good night."

Mr. Elmstruck hung up the phone before I could finish my sentence, but that didn't alarm me at all. I couldn't wait to reunite with him. I texted Amidah and let her know to be at my house by tomorrow morning. I didn't want to tell my mother because I knew she'd throw a fit and probably pull the plug on the party. *He didn't appear dangerous to me*, I thought.

The next day Amidah picked me up to go to Mr. Elmstruck's house. I walked outside in a royal blue dress with white and royal blue shoes. Amidah was surprised when I got in the car.

"Girl, um, you look cute and all, but how did you get past security at 9:00 a.m. with that outfit on? You are still going to the same place, right?"

"Amidah come on." I laughed. "It's a reunion. I wanted to be dressed for the occasion. The last time he saw me, I was just a little kid. I'm a big girl now."

Amidah chuckled but did not utter another word. I could tell that part of her didn't like what I was doing, but as my best friend, the most she could do was support me.

We arrived at the complex. My heart began to beat fast. I began reminiscing about all the memories. So much changed, including the color of the buildings and the small basketball court that used to be in front of his house. The park we used to go to across the street was rebuilt. I didn't expect Amidah to come inside, but she put the car in park and exited the vehicle without me even asking. I was glad she was here.

When we walked to the front of the door, there were two chairs outside and a tray full of cigarettes. The smell of burnt bacon filled the air. I knocked on the door a few times, but there was no answer. I could tell by the look on Amidah's face that she was ready to head back to the car. I stood outside for over five minutes then started ringing the bell. Amidah pressed her car remote to unlock the doors. She began walking back toward the car as I continued to stand at the door, still knocking. I rang the bell one last time. Still no answer. I began walking back to the car right behind her.

As soon as I opened the car door, I saw Mr. Elmstruck walking up a hill with four black bags, two in each hand. He had on black sunglasses, army pants, a tan fitted shirt with a fanny pack, and black combat boots. I immediately slammed the car door and ran up to him.

"Mr. Elmstruck! Mr. Elmstruck!" I exclaimed. He was surprised, almost dropping the bags in his hands. He seemed happy to see me but didn't say a word. He entered the combination code to the lock on the door, which was my birthday.

"Electa, I didn't think you were going to show up," he said.

"We spoke yesterday. Why wouldn't I?" I asked in confusion. Mr. Elmstruck appeared distant. I always remembered him being this way. It was as if he was always in the realm of his own mind and thoughts with not much to say until he had his cup in his hand.

"Are you hungry? I'm making a mean bacon, egg, and cheese sandwich with steak on the side."

"At ten in the morning?" I asked surprisingly.

"Hell yeah!" he shouted.

We spent most of the morning catching up and laughing. He showed me old pictures from when I was little and even shared more pictures of my long-lost brother Samion. There was one particular photo with Samion sitting on Mr. Elmstruck's left leg while his cup was in his other hand. Samion's face looked sad as if whoever took the photo did a good job at stopping him from crying long enough to snap what might have looked like a decent moment between the two.

"Do you still have that favorite cup you always used to drink out of?" I asked hesitantly.

"No, no, I got rid of that stuff. Besides, the doctors have been telling me about my liver and this and that."

"When can I meet him, Mr. Elmstruck?" I asked.

"Meet who? Yo brother? I have no idea. That boy went away a long time ago, Electa. Right after his house burned down. You were about four years old the last time I saw him, and he was about ten. That boy must be going on twenty-two years now."

He got up and started organizing books on a brown shelf with dust all over it.

"Well, you came here all by yourself?" he asked. I could tell he didn't want to get into the details on Samion. Mr. Elmstruck always changed the subject when he didn't want to answer a question or discuss a certain topic.

"Didn't you live there too? How did the house burn down?" I asked. "And no, my best friend, Amidah, came with me. She's waiting in the car."

"All this damn time? Tell her to come in. We have enough food to go around."

"Well," I said reluctantly, "she just texted me that she's back out front. I'm actually going to get going. I just wanted to spend time with you and give you this."

I handed him a white and lavender invitation to my sweet sixteen birthday party next weekend. He slowly stroked the dark purple ribbon on it.

"It would mean a lot to me if you came," I said as I gave him a hug. "I'll call you when I get home."

Mr. Elmstruck walked me to the car. He held my hand as if I was a little kid again. A few men were outside watching me, and I could feel his need to be protective. It felt good to feel protected by him for once, even if it was for a moment. He opened the car door and waved at Amidah. She smiled.

The rest of the car ride was quiet. Amidah played some soul music and didn't say much until we arrived in front of my house.

"Does your mom know, you know, that he's back?"

"No, and she will soon enough. I invited him to the party." Amidah paused and slowly turned her head at me. "He didn't have his cup Amidah and the bags in his hands were food from the corner store and meat market. He doesn't drink anymore."

"That's what he told you?" Amidah asked in disbelief. "Did you look in his fridge?"

I immediately opened the car door and slammed it behind me. I couldn't believe that Amidah didn't bother to ask me how it went. I was beginning to think she wanted me to be father-less. Either that or she wanted to keep parading her perfect dad in my face so I could continue to pretend he was my father too. Amidah was the only child since her twin sister passed away when we were kids. I was the only person closest to a sister she ever had. What mattered most to me was that I spent the whole day with Mr. Elmstruck, and not once did he have his cup in his hand, and that was enough for me to believe him.

The week went by fast. Mr. Elmstruck and I spoke more times that week than Amidah and I did in one month. She and I touched base on things pertaining to the party, but that was about it.

My sweet sixteen birthday party was finally tomorrow, and I couldn't wait to see all my friends from school; family; drama teacher, Mr. Madrid; and our church family. My mother was cooking and prepping most of the food. She made some of my favorite dishes like lasagna and baked mac 'n' cheese. I was hoping to hear back from Amidah since she was responsible for handling the limo, but since my other friend, Graddie, had an uncle who owns a private limo company, he ended up being our limo driver on short notice. Besides, he loved my mother's cooking and only did it for the food.

Friday night was hectic as many people filled our house. My mother and I entertained our guests, and I was happy to be surrounded by the love of friends and family. I hoped Mr. Elmstruck would show. I called his phone twice, but it went straight to voice mail. I left him a message.

The next day everyone was running around preparing for the party. Although it didn't start until 6:00 p.m., there was still a lot to do, and time was moving fast. Amidah texted me throughout the morning, but I could tell she was still upset. My hair was pinned up into curls with a straight bang. I wore a nice purple trumpet dress with a diamond tiara that had the words "Sweet 16 Princess." All my girls were dressed in white, purple, and gold.

After we all finished getting ready, it was time for us to head out to the party. As everyone was going into the limo, Amidah showed up at the very last minute and parked her car. She walked over with a gift in her hand and gave me a hug. "Happy sweet sixteen, Lec. I love you."

When we arrived at the venue, I was in awe with how beautiful the decorations were made from the tablecloths to the dessert table with my three-decker cake. I saw my mother across the room in her beautiful lavender gown lighting scented candles at the gifts table. I began to get teary-eyed at all the work everyone put in to make this day special. Many of my high school friends, teachers, and family came. The DJ was spinning the best songs, and everyone was dancing and enjoying themselves.

A couple hours passed since the party started. After pictures were taken, food was eaten, and it began to get late, I couldn't help but wonder where Mr. Elmstruck was. It was already eleven at night, and the party was scheduled to end at eleven thirty. Amid how hectic things were, I went to the ladies' room to call him but still no answer. I left another voicemail, hoping he didn't hear me struggling to hold back my tears.

Suddenly, the bathroom door flew open, and I could hear all the commotion as people prepared to dance to the "Cha Cha Slide." No one knew I was in the stall. I could tell from the voices that entered that it was my godmother, Mary Lou, and one of my mother's best friends, Remee, who rushed in. They seemed disturbed.

"Mary Lou are you going to tell her? I got twenty-twenty vision, and I can't forget the devil! How many times do I have to tell you that when I went out to smoke my cigarette, I saw that man fall out of the taxi cab? I don't even think he paid. That's how much the poor guy wanted to drop his behind off!"

Remee shook her head. "We have to tell her. This is such an important birthday to Electa, and to see them so happy, I'd hate for this ambush to ruin everything. How did he know about this party anyway? It's been well over eight years since—"

As Remee was talking, the door slammed open again, but this time it was my mother.

"Where the hell is Electa!" she yelled. "And who invited that monster to our family event!" No one said a word. Her hands began trembling. I wanted to walk out of the stall but froze. More relatives and friends came into the bathroom looking for me, including myself. They all came together to figure out how to get rid of Mr. Elmstruck and his special guest—the cup in his hand.

The music stopped playing, and once everyone left the restroom, I walked out slowly to find Mr. Elmstruck eating through my cake with his bare hands. The DJ was no longer playing music, and I saw four of my older male cousins run back in to restrain him.

"Wher…Where's my baby!" he yelled in an innocent but slurred voice as the men sought to escort him out.

"What are you little punks doing! You motherfuckers can't hurt me! You know who I am!" shouted Mr. Elmstruck. He managed to get loose from the men but then suddenly tripped over a few cords connected to the DJ's sound equipment. When he fell by the dessert table, some of the food in glassware shattered on the floor, along with some decorative vases.

I stood there and watched as my mother fell into tears. Some people were so afraid that Mr. Elmstruck would attack them, so they decided to leave immediately. Before anyone could call the police, Mr. Elmstruck vanished into the night.

It was like Cinderella left her shoe, but instead it was a trail of blood leading to outside. I found a medium-size sixteen-ounce coffee cup on the floor. It must've spilled when Mr. Elmstruck fell right by the stairs at the entrance. I picked the cup up and threw it in the trash. There were no more ounces left in it to drink. My mother watched me from across the dance floor. I could feel her piercing dark brown eyes look down on me with disgust. She wouldn't speak to me, but I knew that based on my reaction, she was able to connect this to being all my fault.

An awkward silence filled the room. The DJ's sound system was not working since Mr. Elmstruck caused a short fuse when some of the drinks fell. When the DJ walked up to me, I was hoping he didn't expect to sing "Happy Birthday." There was nothing happy about it, and no one wanted to sing.

"Just so y'all know, it's 11:20 p.m., and it's gonna take me about twenty more minutes to pack up, so y'all still gotta pay for the time, along with these damages to my sound system.

I know some random drunk bum got in here, but the contract says—"

"I don't need you to explain to me what the contract says!" I shouted. It was the first words I said since Mr. Elmstruck entered that door with his cup.

"Pack up and leave, young man. We'll be in touch," said my godmother, Mary Lou, hastily.

I left and went outside for some air. I saw Amidah putting some of my birthday gifts in her car. "Your mom asked me to bring you home. Graddie's uncle already picked up Graddie and the other girls. Are you ready?" she asked. I nodded and went inside the car. The awkward silence in the party must have followed us there because Amidah and I didn't speak either.

Three months had passed since my mother spoke to me in the house. She wasn't the type to vocalize her feelings and often internalized everything. Her silence was enough to let me know that she had a lot of questions that only I had the answers to. Mr. Elmstruck, on the other hand, persistently called, texted, and left me messages, but I couldn't find it in me to return any of his calls. The last message he sent me asked if I could stop by his place so that we could talk. He apparently couldn't remember anything from my birthday party and was wondering why I wasn't returning any of his calls.

The next day I woke up to soft rock music playing and the smell of sausages, pancakes, and eggs. The only time I smelled food and heard music was when my mother was in a great mood. *She's finally over it*, I thought. Today was the day I finally took my road test. I went downstairs where my mother was eating breakfast with a man I had never seen before. There was a bouquet of lavender roses and lily blooms on the table. The man quickly jumped with his hand out as if he didn't expect me to be home. He looked like someone from a car commercial trying to sell his last car on the lot.

"Hi, Electa, my name is Leon. Your mother has told me so much about you. It's a pleasure to finally meet you." He put his hand down when he noticed I didn't show much enthusiasm and resumed putting fruit in my mother's bowl.

"Thanks," I replied. I grabbed my keys and walked toward the door. "I'm catching the bus to go take my road test, Mom!" I shouted. I walked back toward the kitchen and realized that my mother paid me no mind. She laughed hysterically as her handyman continued to feed her strawberries with whipped cream.

My phone rang. I thought it was Amidah, but it was Mr. Elmstruck. He left me another message saying that he needed to see me urgently because he wasn't feeling too well. As much as I wanted to hate him for what he'd done at my birthday party, I still cared enough to know what was wrong.

## chapter four

# TWENTY OUNCES

As years went by, the relationship I had with my mother became more estranged while Mr. Elmstruck and I grew closer together. Although he traveled back and forth from the military, we continued to write and stay in touch. My mother and I rarely spoke, but when we did, it was mainly for me to check on my four-year-old brother Cadence.

After dating my mom for a couple of months, Leon moved in and married her shortly thereafter. We didn't get along much, and I ended up living on campus by the time I graduated from high school. By the age of twenty, I had my own apartment, car and finished college with a four-year degree in psychology. I took a few college accelerated classes to graduate early in high school and finished college earlier so that I could work out in the field sooner.

On the days I wasn't working, I'd visit Mr. Elmstruck and his mother. He hadn't been the same since his twin sister, Arlena, became ill four years before, which led to her admittance to a nursing facility. They were very close, and she kept him out of a lot of trouble even though she, too, had a cup in her hand every once in a while.

One day Mr. Elmstruck took a turn for the worse when he got a phone call from his sister's nurse that she might not make it and needed to be transferred to the intensive care unit for twenty-four-hour monitoring. He stayed in his room with the door locked and wept. Ms. Elmstruck did everything she could to try to engage him, but nothing would make him come out of that room, not even to use the bathroom. He called me while I was at work and left me a voice message. I could tell from the sadness in his voice that he needed me to go and support my aunt. She and I were very close when I was younger. After work, I drove to the facility where Aunt Arlena was. When I entered the building, I saw two nurses sitting at the front desk, one of which instantly recognized who I was. The nurse, Darline, was fond of Mr. Elmstruck and my aunt, so she allowed me to go into the room where my aunt lay in a coma.

I walked into the room and became overwhelmed with emotion. As I walked slowly toward the bed, I could see how pale and peaceful she looked as if she was awaiting to leave her sorrows behind her. I gently rubbed my hand on hers in a circular motion as tears flowed down both my cheeks.

"Auntie Arlena, I don't know if you could hear me, but I want to say thank you for everything you've done for me. I wish I could have more time with you, especially with all of the gaps in years I wasn't able to spend with you. I remember how you taught me how to play pool and ride my first tricycle. Or the times when you would take me out to the forest behind your house and gather hard oak or maple wood for the fireplace."

I paused as I felt a slight movement from her finger, but she still lay in a motionless state.

"Remember how you used to teach me how to cook rice even though you never liked to put salt in yours?" I laughed. "I hope you make it out of this. If you don't, please watch over us, especially my dad. If there's anyone who never judged him and always had his back, it's you. No one else understands him better than you did, and without you, he's lost. I—"

Before I could finish my sentence, the door opened, and I thought it was Nurse Darline, but it was someone else.

"I'm sorry to interrupt. Nurse Darline said another relative was here. I thought you were her elder daughter, Shelly."

The young man had a fresh line up. His mustache and beard were full. He wore a shirt that had the logo of the local community center, along with gray basketball shorts. I could tell by his physique and the sneakers he wore that he probably played sports often and went to the gym.

I quickly wiped my tears and turned around to see the face to whom the deep manly voice belonged.

"Uh, hi. Darline said no one else could be in here but family. Are you her son or…?"

The young man chuckled.

"I guess you could say. My mother passed away from lung cancer, and as for my father, he wasn't in a stable mind space to raise me, so she's been my mother and father since I was a young bull in diapers. Sorry, I'm her nephew. My name is Samion. You?"

For a second, it seemed like the world stopped moving. I couldn't believe my elder brother Samion was in the flesh looking right at me after all these years. For a moment, I felt disgusted with myself for finding my own brother attractive.

"Samion?" I asked. "I'm Electa, your younger sister."

"Electa as in 'my father's other daughter from another mother' Electa? Come here, nugget. I can't believe this! Man, Auntie Arlena would have wanted this. We have so much to catch up on. My phone is in my car, but if you have yours, I can give you my number. Text me so I know it's you."

We continued to talk for over an hour as our aunt lay still and listened. There were moments where I could see a slight smile on her face, and Samion and I both agreed that somehow it was her way of letting us know that she could hear us. My phone rang, and it was Mr. Elmstruck. I pressed decline and continued to talk to my big brother, Samion, whom I spent years without.

"I know there's a lot of questions you have, Electa, like where I've been and why I haven't been around. I owe you that explanation, and I would rather you hear it from me. I have a game later today. Can we have lunch after this?" Samion asked.

"Yes, Samion, sure. There's a diner not too far from here." We each kissed our aunt Arlena with the hope that she'd be awake by tomorrow.

Samion followed my car to a diner that I used to go to with Mr. Elmstruck when I was little. He loved going to that place because there was a liquor store next door to it that he'd stop at before and after our little lunch outings. Samion seemed very serious like there was more he wanted to tell me but couldn't in the intensive care unit. At least he had enough respect for our aunt to not let her know what she already knew about Mr. Elmstruck.

We sat down at a table, and I couldn't help but look at how much my brother resembled Mr. Elmstruck.

"Electa, I know I can't use this time to make up for the years of my absence in your life. Before Auntie Arlena got sick, she told me that you and our dad reconnected. I'm happy for you, but I just can't say the same for myself. I've been going to therapy since I was a kid. I can count on one hand how many times I've seen him since I moved in with Auntie Arlena."

The waitress came to our table to take our order. I could tell by the look in her eyes that she would put Samion on the menu if he gave her the time and day.

"I'll have a strawberry lemonade with extra strawberries, a BLT, and extra avocado on the side. Thank you." The woman smiled as she wrote down his order, and somehow her enthusiasm disappeared when it was time to ask me for mine.

"Here's the menu, hun. I'll have what my brother is having. Oh, and it doesn't cost to smile," I said sarcastically. The woman gave a weird look as she took the menus and walked away.

"Awkward, Lec. What was that all about?" asked Samion.

"Oh, nothing. Just already annoyed that my brother is a ladies' magnet, nothing serious."

We both laughed, and I could tell Samion was happy to see me. We realized that even though we spent years apart growing up in two different worlds, we were a lot alike.

"What happened to you, guys?" I asked. "I mean, you don't have to tell me everything. But you mentioned back at the hospital that you'd never see him ever again."

I could tell Samion didn't want to talk about it, but he knew it was an important piece for me to understand him. I gently held his hand, consoling him and showing that he could trust me.

"Every time he had that cup, he used to beat me...a lot, Electa, to the point where I couldn't eat or sleep. Sometimes I'd lie awake at night just to make sure I was ready for when he came stumbling in my room, roughing me up about how I ain't shit and how he asked my mom to abort me 'cause he wasn't sure if I was his or the doctor she worked closely with." Samion paused. He looked away, and his eyes were filled with tears. Not one rolled down.

"I'm so sorry, Samion. I didn't know," I said sadly. "All these years I always asked about you, but I could never get a clear answer. Besides, the two times I saw you years ago at Auntie Arlena's house, I figured everything was okay."

"For a long time, no one didn't know this but my mom. She worked long days and nights as a nurse for weeks at a time. I barely saw her. He used to hit her too, of course, only when he had his cup in his hand, so she was afraid to even confront him about it. One day he was so drunk that he fell asleep and left the stove on."

"Do you know how the fire started?" I asked.

"Yeah. He was frying a damn twenty-ounce rib eye steak on high heat that eventually dried out, caught on fire and burned the whole house down. Luckily my mom always taught me survival skills, so I was able to make a run for it through the fire escape and go to our neighbor's house next door. Lec, I was hoping he died in that fire, but even hell didn't want him." I didn't know what to say.

Samion excused himself and went to the restroom. I could tell it was hard for him because as he relived the moments, his body language seemed unnerving. I wanted to ask him if his mother's death had anything to do with the fire but I figured that was a conversation for another time. Once our food came out, I waited for a couple of minutes. After some time I noticed that Samion was taking long. I began to eat my food.

"Sorry about that, Electa. I grabbed my phone from the car. Shelly called me a few times, so I called her back to let her know the status of Auntie Arlena. She handles all of the legality and medical stuff, so we were just touching base. Where was I?"

"About to eat, bro! Come on, we have time to catch up. Put something in your stomach," I said eagerly.

We joked around about different things we liked to do and some of our most outrageous past relationship experiences. I told him about an ex whom I had to run away from, and he told me about an ex who would jump out the bushes every week by the gym he worked out in just to "run into him again."

Part of me felt bad for Mr. Elmstruck. I wanted to help him, but the more I learned, the more I realized that maybe there was a reason why he didn't want me to know anything about Samion. After lunch, Samion and I went our separate ways. He planned for me, him, and Shelly to meet at Auntie Arlena's house for dinner tomorrow night.

Once I left the diner, I called Mr. Elmstruck to make sure he was feeling better. He always became really dismissive and angry when he didn't get a response from me right away.

"Hello!" he shouted on the phone.

"Hi, Mr. Elmstruck," I said.

"Why the hell do you call me that, Electa! I'm your father! And I've been calling you all goddamn day so I can talk to my sister because I can't go see her like that! You know what? I'm out."

The phone suddenly hung up. I became used to Mr. Elmstruck's outbursts, especially when he didn't get his way. Normally I would be flustered, but this time, after reconnecting with my big brother and seeing my auntie Arlena, there was a level of happiness I felt big enough to help me disregard his negativity.

When I got home, I texted Amidah about the great news. She couldn't wait to meet my big brother, Samion. I was glad to have my best friend's support because she knew how important it was for me to reconnect with my family and also help Mr. Elmstruck. The more I studied addiction and came into contact with others who experienced it, the more eager I became in trying to understand Mr. Elmstruck and his drunken woes.

The next day was Friday. I tried to call Mr. Elmstruck a few times, but he didn't answer or return any of my calls. I left him a message in hopes that he would call me back and I could visit him. When I arrived at Aunt Arlena's house, Samion answered the door.

"Hey, hey, hey, little sister!" he exclaimed. "Come on in. Shelly and I cheffed it up. Let me hang your stuff up. Have a seat in the dining room. Shelly is just setting up," he said. He took my coat as I walked toward the dining room. I was amazed at how many family photos she had. I even found two pictures of me, one where I was standing by the stairs in my two pigtails and another was of her holding me when I was a baby.

"My, my, my, if it isn't my lovely little cousin! You've grown!" said Shelly as she rushed over to give me a hug. "The Lord is so good. It's great to see you."

"Thank you, Shelly. I was telling Samion how much I always thought of him and would draw pictures of us in my sketchbook when I was a little kid. I asked my father for him when we reconnected, but he never says much, if anything, at all."

Samion walked in the room with a few dishes. "Well, Electa, I didn't mention that after the fire, Aunt Arlena took me in, and after that I never really spoke to him again. She tried to bring him around a few times, but that was about it."

"Yeah, a few times turned into none!" joked Shelly. "You may not know, but your father and that cup is something dangerous, Electa. You never questioned why he never came to graduations, birthdays, and family functions?"

I hesitated to speak because although Mr. Elmstruck had his cup, he was still my father, and part of helping him didn't mean putting his demons on display. "Well, I heard things from my mom and other family members on his side, but I never really knew what the truth was."

"That's fair," said Samion as he passed me Shelly's squash casserole.

"Electa, I could tell by the look on your face that you don't want to hear the truth about your father, do you?" asked Shelly.

"No, it's not that, Shelly. Since him and I reconnected, I've been trying to deal with him and the truth, and it's just been…you know…a little hard to take in. He doesn't open up to me."

"I understand," said Shelly. "Look, I'm here to get to know you better. All these years went by and you didn't know your family because his own family disowned him because of his drinking. I won't get into it too much, but I'm thirty-six years old. The memories of an Uncle constantly being drunk and groping you at twelve, then fifteen is not easy to shake. Especially when he denies it because he doesn't remember it even happened."

When Shelly told us what Mr. Elmstruck did, I sat there quietly and asked myself, *"If he had too much to drink and kept refilling his favorite cup to no return, would he touch me?"* As I stared into a trance, Samion nudged me.

"Earth to Lecky! Dang, girl, wake up." He laughed. "I mean, we grew from a lot of that pain. We aren't trying to convince you 'cause clearly you're grown and have to set your own path. We just don't think it's a good idea to reunite with him, and maybe you haven't seen enough for you to make that decision. But let's eat and dance 'cause we have a lot to celebrate. I won nationals yesterday, and I got my baby sister back in my life."

It began to get late. I didn't want to go to Mr. Elmstruck's house, especially around this time because he normally was up at night with his cup. After helping Shelly and Samion clean up, I drove to Mr. Elmstruck's house anyway. The little girl in me felt bad and wanted to help him even though the truth was that Mr. Elmstruck only caused more ounces of tears than the bottles and beer cans he drank.

As I was passing the local liquor store not too far from his house, I saw a lot of commotion outside with the owner and a few other guys. I suddenly saw Mr. Elmstruck get pushed out while yelling curse words and refusing to leave. There were no parking spaces available, but I was able to find a spot by a fire hydrant. I wasn't expecting to be long and ran across the street to get Mr. Elmstruck.

"I can go wherever the hell I want to, boy!" he yelled in a slurred voice. As soon as I approached the men, the owner walked back over to us.

"Is this your old man?" he asked. "Get his butt out of here before my guys rip him apart. He's been banned from my store, and he knows it." Another man on a motorcycle approached us. He had on black sunglasses, a tattoo on his neck that said, "Die slowly," and combat boots with a black leather vest on.

He lowered his glasses gently, so I could see that he only had one eye. "Young lady, take him home, please. We've already whooped his ass once. The next time will be the last, if you know what I mean. And this here ain't a threat. It's a warning." He spat on the side twice.

I quickly grabbed Mr. Elmstruck's arm from the front of the entrance as he stumbled back and forth. He ended up walking around the corner out of sight. I went to look for him, but I couldn't tell which way he turned. I looked back and saw more men idling by the liquor store. As I was walking, trying not to cause a scene, I saw another liquor store a few blocks away. When I ran in there, Mr. Elmstruck was arguing with the clerk as to why they couldn't sell him any more liquor.

"Boy, let me get a taste right now!" he shouted. "Or I'll break your motherfuc—"

"Dad! Please stop!" shouted the little girl inside me.

"Mami, take your papa away. I can't sell him anything when he's like that. He is a good guy but not when he is like this. *No Bueno*," said the man in Spanish.

Mr. Elmstruck finally decided to give up. Each time I tried to take ahold of his arm, he yanked it away from me. We managed to walk back, and my car was being towed. The hydrant was turned on, and I had a feeling it was the biker dude's way of letting me know we didn't belong there.

"Please, I had to find my dad. He's not in a place to care for himself right now, and I have no way of getting back home. It's a far drive." The man took off his headphones. I could tell he heard nothing I just said but could see from my watery eyes that I couldn't let him take my car.

"Sorry, lady, this car is not supposed to be parked here, and the fire department is on their way in less than five minutes," said the tow truck driver, putting his headphones back on and continuing to bob his head.

Mr. Elmstruck began walking in the direction of his house. The boys across the street began whistling and blowing kisses at me. Even the biker guy with the one eye lowered his glasses back down to give me a wink from the one eye he had.

"Um, fine. I'll just pick it up tomorrow," I said to the tow driver.

"No problem, lady. Cowers Towing. Were only about five minutes away. We open tomorrow from 7:00 a.m. to 4:00 p.m. Don't be late. And it's one hundred bucks plus an additional fifty dollars storage fee if you don't show up."

I watched the driver leave with my car strapped right on it. I turned, and Mr. Elmstruck was gone. I began running and saw him walk across the busy streets looking straight ahead. It was like he lost full control of his ability to listen to his own conscience. Cars honked as he continued to walk through busy intersections. At one point, one car drove into a pole to avoid hitting him. He continued to stumble and walk. There was a short pathway he always took that led him to the back of his house quicker. It was a dirt area with tall grass.

"Wait! Mr. Elmstruck!" I shouted. "Dad!" He turned around briefly and yelled back at me.

"What is it! What is it!" he shouted. "What do you want!" He continued to stumble in the streets until he tripped over a boulder and fell. I took out my small flashlight so I could see in the darkness. He sat on the dirt ground slouched over, breathing heavily.

"Let's go!" I yelled. "It's dark, and we have ten more min-utes left to get you safely to the house."

I could hear him mumbling, but no words were coming from his mouth, just a whole bunch of excessive saliva and spit. After standing there for ten minutes, my feet began to hurt from walking. I sat right beside him and watched him as he leaned over to his left and dozed in and out of sleep. I couldn't call anyone for help because everyone warned me about Mr. Elmstruck and his cup.

There was a bus stop right on the main street. A bus was coming from afar, and in the midst of me thinking about what I was going to do, Mr. Elmstruck attempted to place his right hand between my legs. I pushed him and stood.

"Are you serious, Mr. Elmstruck!" I screamed. "I hate you, and I'm never speaking to you ever again!"

He lay in the dirt. I couldn't tell if he was dead or alive, but it didn't even matter to me anymore. The bus stopped at a red light. I could feel a deep lump in my throat as I fought to hold back my tears. *How can he do this to me?* I thought. I was too scared to walk back and see if the driver who crashed into the pole was dead. After all, Mr. Elmstruck wouldn't remember any of this in the morning. I ran to the bus while he lay hopelessly on the ground.

When I got home that night, I took a long shower. I had several missed calls and texts but couldn't respond to any of them because I was distraught and broken. The last thing I needed to hear was "I told you so." I put on my pajamas and took out my phone. I knew Mr. Elmstruck couldn't have made it home yet. He was too out of it to even move his leg. I called the house phone and left a message.

"*Mr. Elmstruck, by tomorrow you won't remember anything that happened tonight, so I'll leave a recording that can remind you. Tonight, you violated me. You were so drunk that not only did you embarrass me and almost get us killed, but you made me look at you in a way I never thought I would! The same dark light everyone else sees you in when you've had too much to drink. You need help. Never would I suspect you to try and put your hands between my legs. A father protects his children, not puts them in harm's way! Ever!*" I hung up and began to cry as my tears found their way outside of me.

The next morning I called out of work so that I could pick up my car from the towing company and recuperate from everything that transpired from the night before. Mr. Elmstruck continuously kept calling and leaving messages that I didn't care to return. I could see he was still alive and got my message. I wondered how someone could apologize for something they say they don't remember. I was just thankful that the news reported that the driver who ran into the pole suffered minor injuries and a small scratch on his forehead. The driver did not remember what happened but told authorities that a pedestrian stumbled in the street, and he swerved to avoid hitting him. No charges were made.

After a week, I felt like I was finally getting back to my happy self. I no longer trusted Mr. Elmstruck but it didn't change how much I wished I could help him.

My phone had several alerts. Shelly texted me to let me know that she received a call from another family member stating that Mr. Elmstruck had abandoned his home for a few days. He pushed one of the prostitutes he picked up from the street down the stairs after finishing the last drop of the three forty-ounce bottles he drank that night.

It all made sense why Shelly would often laugh that the universe always had a way of working in his favor. Mr. Elmstruck was never arrested for the assault, which probably had a lot to do with his connections in the court system and the fact that his mother would never let him go to jail. She lied to the police and told them that the woman was a coke addict attempting to steal from the house and upon running away, fell down the stairs.

I changed my number and distanced myself from Mr. Elmstruck for what would be the longest time we'd ever been apart from each other.

## chapter five

# FORTY OUNCES

The spring rain beat steadily on the long glass windows. I had just finished wrapping up my last-minute meeting with a new psychologist who specializes in working with clients with long-term substance abuse. Omah, along with two counselors and a coordinator, was the last piece to make this dream team a reality.

After many years of sacrifices and dedication, I finally achieved my goal of opening my own counseling clinic. It was the Friday before the weekend when I drove to the brick building to make sure everything was in place and ready for opening week.

"It was a pleasure to meet you, Omah," I said pleasantly while walking her to the door. "I'll have a full schedule ready for you first thing on Monday." Omah stopped at the front entrance, holding the doorknob. She turned around slowly and placed her hand gently on my shoulder.

"Thank you, Mrs. E. I can't wait to have some of my old clients come back. Some haven't been the same since I left my old job, and they count on me to help them through their tough times. They're what keeps me going, you know?" said Omah.

"I hear you," I replied. "And this place will always be a safe haven for any person who walks through that door, no matter what. It means more to me that people see this as a home, not a recovery clinic that teaches them how to suppress their demons."

After I let Omah out, I sat on the beige multicolored flower couch reminiscing on how far I'd come after receiving my PhD in psychology. It was a struggle financially because right before I purchased my house with my husband, Neil, Ms. Elmstruck's health took a toll for the worse, and she needed someone to help with keeping up with all her medical costs. I didn't see her but sent monthly payments of $500 to Nurse Darline, who became a family friend honoring Aunt Arlena's wishes.

Mr. Elmstruck was nowhere to be found, and word on the street was that he was shacking up at a lady friend's house somewhere in the inner city. Every now and then, he'd send letters to my mother's old apartment, where we all used to live. Our kind neighbors would bring those letters to her until one day she sent one back to him with a note that said, "Electa hasn't lived here in over twenty-four years. Go write to your cup instead."

It took a while for my mother to forgive me for letting Mr. Elmstruck in behind her back, but I knew a huge part of her was angrier that she couldn't do anything about it. Luckily Neil was a family man and great supporter. He was no stranger to family dysfunction himself, so he did what he could to help me cope. We'd been married for over ten years now and had handsome twin boys, Eyan and Sanil. Sanil reminded me a lot of my brother Samion, who was the first one to tell me I was pregnant with twins before any of us knew. It felt good to have a positive role model for the boys to look up to other than their father.

Neil worked as a biomedical engineer and just started his own manufacturing company, so we decided to celebrate both our achievements along with the boys' birthdays that upcoming weekend. My mother and Samion were going to be staying at our house while Shelly planned to fly in tomorrow with her husband and three daughters. When Aunt Arlena died a few years ago, Shelly ended up renting out the house and moving to another state. Samion got married and moved into his own home with his daughter, Sulaay.

As I was organizing the waiting area and putting magazines in a basket, a couple of mail dropped through the door mail slot. Most of it was junk, but there was one particular letter that had my maiden name. When I opened it, it read:

*Miss Electa,*

*I would call you, but I don't have your number and you probably wouldn't accept any calls from me anyway. You're probably wondering how I got this address? Well. I had one of my buddies over at a sheriff's department look it up and wanted to make sure this letter got to you around the time your clinic opened. I'm so proud of you baby! I know I ain't been there but I'm still your father. The one and only. You only have one. I hope we have a chance to talk soon. How's everything with ya? I hope you ain't got no damn boyfriend yet. I'm really sorry for the way things went down between us. You said I touched something, but I don't remember that. I said I was sorry. Can I see you soon? It would mean so much to me. Give me a call when you get a chance. I wrote my number on the back of this letter.*

*Love,*

*Your Beloved Father E. Elmstruck*

A small tear trickled down my right cheek. Many years have passed since Mr. Elmstruck and I wrote to one another. I could always tell his letters from his handwriting. No one wrote like him. His words were written in all bold, italic caps. I felt a sense of hope for his recovery after seeing that he was still alive.

When I got home, the house was quiet. I walked up the stairs and saw a trail of roses leading into the bathroom. I opened the door and walked into a steam-filled room with lavender scent and a candlelight bubble bath. There was a silver platter on top of the bathroom sink that had a plate full of fruits, along with my favorite glass of red wine. Next to it was a small note written on lavender paper that read, "Unwind in fizzy bubbles my Queen." I couldn't help but chuckle. Neil was the only one who knew that I used the term "fizzy" for bubbles because it reminded me of the ounces in Mr. Elmstruck's cup. It was Neil's way of making me smile after a long day.

After my bath, I slipped right under the covers beside him. He was already asleep, and I didn't want to wake him. I was sure he had a long day between entertaining the kids and preparing the house for tomorrow. I couldn't stop thinking about Mr. Elmstruck's letter and couldn't help but cry silently under the sheets. I wanted to tell Neil about the letter, but I knew what he was going to say, and the last thing I'd want was for Mr. Elmstruck to unleash on the one man I knew he couldn't beat even on a sober day.

"Whatever is bothering you, my love, let's talk about it after this weekend. But get some rest 'cause we have a long day ahead," Neil whispered as he snuggled behind me. I almost forgot that this man could spot my pain a mile away, especially when I was close. I kissed his muscular arms and drifted off to sleep.

At eight o'clock the next morning, I was greeted by my energetic niece, Sulaay. Neil was already downstairs making breakfast.

"You're still sleeping, Lec!" shouted my mom as she stood by the bedroom door. At sixty-three, she still had that sharp, authoritative tone like she would put you over her lap for a spanking anytime.

"No, ma'am, I'm up now," I said with sarcasm and excitement at the same time. "Mamaaa, come give me a hug!" I yelled as I ran up to her and grabbed her things. The boys were happy to see her too.

We spent most of the day laughing and talking about old memories and looking at family photos in my album. I was in a daze watching my brother and niece dance to a nice rhythm and blues playlist compiled by Neil. My mother sat on the opposite side of the room quietly staring at a picture in her hand. Her face had no expression, but I knew my mother. I could tell from where I was sitting that the back of the photo read, "Forever my lavender loves 6.3.94." She slowly put the photograph back in the pocket of my *Family Memories* photo album and placed it under the couch.

The doorbell rang. It was Shelly, her husband, and three daughters. They made it just in time for our family dinner. Neil finished preparing the table, and I instantly stood and walked to the kitchen when I heard the sound of Shelly's voice.

"Electa, you stuck your foot in this cinnamon apple pie!" yelled Shelly.

"Her foot, head, and toes!" Samion said, laughing.

"I'd like to make a toast," said Shelly's husband, Jim, as he began pouring a vintage red wine brought back from their vineyard.

"To family, unity, and always sticking together. May we have more moments and memories that we are able to share with one another."

We all tapped glasses and ended the night with karaoke. The next day was the boys' fifth birthday. Neil, Samion, and Jim got the grill and speakers ready as the rest of us made our way to the pool and water slide bouncy house.

As we were enjoying ourselves, my mother walked over to me with the same photograph from last night. Mr. Elmstruck's face was cut out of it.

"Electa," she said in a stern voice, "I hope you don't deal with that jerk and sorry piece of excuse of a human being. Live your life. Don't let this man and his cup get in the way of everything you worked hard to achieve I'd hate to see him hurt you...again."

I didn't know what to say to my mother other than to nod and give her a hug. Even in his absence, Mr. Elmstruck somehow brought tears to our eyes. Shelly and Samion had already told me last month that they hoped I wasn't planning on providing rehabilitation support for Mr. Elmstruck because he was a useless pot of damaged goods.

After we sang "Happy Birthday" to the boys, we all sat for a nice evening around the firepit. As we were reminiscing on the good times, the house phone kept ringing continuously until finally Neil went to go pick it up.

"Hello. What!" he exclaimed. "Hold on, let me get Electa."

Without alarming our guests, Neil walked back to the yard and got my attention. I could tell by his face that something was wrong.

"Omah called and said she's been trying to reach you since earlier today. Apparently a drunk passed out in his vomit and is lying in his own piss right now, right in front of the clinic." I could tell Neil was upset, but at that moment I just didn't have the right words to say.

"Electa, there's only one drunk I know of that would be laid out in front of your place of business. How long have you been in contact with Mr. Elmstruck? Your grand opening is tomorrow. How in the world did he know where to go? I'm asking too many questions with no answers, Electa." I didn't say a word and continued to stare blankly. Neil walked away and left the phone on the counter. I snapped out of it.

"Omah, what the hell happened!" I asked as I walked over to the dining room. "I'm with my family, and it's the twins' birthday. We haven't even cut the cake yet." I peeked toward the kitchen to make sure no one was listening. "Omah, please don't tell me it's my father." There was a pause on the phone. Omah knew about Mr. Elmstruck a few years ago when we met at a convention raising awareness for those affected by alcohol abuse. I should've known that Mr. Elmstruck would show up unannounced once he knew where to find me.

"I know, I know," said Omah. "I got the call from Raul. While he was finishing some last-minute touches on the door hinges, he heard a loud bang outside. I gotta go, but if you can come down, please do, Electa." I hung up the phone and grabbed the car keys. It was time for me to face Mr. Elmstruck and his cup once and for all.

When I arrived in front of the building, Mr. Elmstruck had just woken up. He looked confused as he tossed in his vomit, trying to gather himself together. I noticed that the empty cup at the bottom of the last stair wasn't a plastic, styrofoam or coffee cup he usually had when he was drinking in the street. There was a forty-ounce bottle shattered into pieces where the chrysanthemums were sprouting. I took a deep breath, turned the car off, and grabbed some maze out of the glove compartment. The door opened, and Omah walked out with Raul standing on the side like he was a bodyguard of some sort.

"Excuse me, sir, are you okay? Do you need us to call the EMT?" Omah asked with a concerned and frightened look. Mr. Elmstruck began mumbling and grunting, but no words were coming out of his mouth.

"Umm…who the hell are you to ask me questions!" he shouted.

"Well, I work here, so can I ask why you are lying in a puddle of vomit while there's a broken bottle in our garden? This is a place of business, and I'm going to have to ask you to leave," said Raul in an assertive tone.

Raul began to crack his neck left and right. I exited my vehicle and walked up to the building. The smell alone was difficult to bear, but it didn't bother Mr. Elmstruck. It looked like he didn't even notice it.

"Mr. El…I mean, Dad," I said hesitantly. The moment he heard my voice, he sat up straight and opened his eyes as big as an owl.

"Is that my baby?" he asked in a high-pitched voice. His bottom lip was busted, and he had some cuts on his arms that were still bleeding. He moved his hands slowly and I could tell they were a little swollen.

"Not a baby anymore." I chuckled. "I'm a forty-year-old woman, Dad. What are you doing here?" I asked.

"I haven't seen you in many years."

"Let's get you cleaned up and talk inside. We have a small shower room with extra clothes and towels."

Raul and Omah had a peculiar look on their faces and didn't understand why the authorities weren't already alerted. Mr. Elmstruck attempted to stand as he began to walk up the remainder of the stairs with a limp. I held his left arm until we entered inside.

"I'm going to get ready to go so I can get rest and prepare for the week. I guess I'll talk to you tomorrow?" asked Omah.

"Yes, I'll take it from here," I said as I cleaned Mr. Elmstruck's wounds with peroxide. After Raul cleaned up the shattered glass and vomit on the stairs, he walked over to hand Mr. Elmstruck his cup.

"Leave it on the table, boy," said Mr. Elmstruck.

He sat quietly on the couch, staring at his favorite cup. After all these years, the stainless silver cup was the closest thing that he kept by his side. It was rare for Mr. Elmstruck to bring this particular cup outside. When he wasn't drinking, he usually kept it on the football coaster on top of the draw in his bedroom. Any cup with liquor was his favorite but this cup was the most special.

Mr. Elmstruck looked tired. There were a couple of gray hairs in his beard. His skin had scaly patches that he often scratched. He wasn't as buff and appeared to have lost a lot of weight.

I placed the towel and washcloth on the table by his cup. "Here are some clothes, Dad."

"Electa, you really don't have to do this," he said.

"I know, but I want to. Besides, you still haven't told me what you're doing here and why you passed out with a broken forty-ounce bottle in my garden. I think I have the right to know, Dad."

Mr. Elmstruck cleared his throat and took the items from the table. He walked over to the shower room and closed the door. While he was showering, the doorbell rang. It was Samion.

"Did you get any of my calls or text, Lec?" he asked. "Neil told me what happened, and I couldn't get on an airplane tonight without making sure my baby sis is okay. Is he still here?"

"Shhh, Samion," I said as I let him in. Samion looked around suspiciously and sat.

"Lec, why is he here? After all these years and the damage he's done to you and this family. Why do you still care to help him, Lec?"

I walked over to Samion and sat right beside him.

"Samion, I spent most of my forty years of life without a father. We can't blame Dad for what happened in the past. And we can't blame him for how he chooses to cope with the pain on his own. We have each other. He has no one. He's here because he needs help, and I understand that now. You should too."

Samion took Mr. Elmstruck's cup.

"You see this, Lec? This is all he cares about. You remind me so much of my mom. She cared just like you until she died shortly after that fire because of him and his stupid cup! And I won't lose you too."

We both heard the doorknob turn. Mr. Elmstruck came out with tears in his eyes. He limped toward us as Samion moved to the next couch.

"My one and only son, I know you hate me. You have all the right to. Never forget I'm your father! Me! And I will always be your father, boy!" yelled Mr. Elmstruck.

"Electa, call me when you put the trash out. I gotta go," said Samion as he grabbed his coat and left. Mr. Elmstruck looked over to me.

"Lec, I came here because I wanted to see you. A friend of mine is trying to get me into this program, and they pay you to complete it. I won't be able to drink, so I had a little taste last night. I guess I must've come here."

"A little?" I said. "And are you doing this for money, Dad, or because you want the help?"

"Electa, I don't need help. I'm fine. Wherever I am and wherever you are, never forget that I love you." I could tell by his trembling hands that he was still hurt by what Samion said. I walked over to my desk and took one of my cards. Mr. Elmstruck was already at the door, about to walk out.

"Wait, Dad. I want to give you something." I handed him the card while still holding on tightly to his bruised hands. "You may not think you need help, but deep down inside I know it's what will help set you free. If that program doesn't work out, I want you to come back here only if you're ready to be sober and heal." He didn't say a word.

Mr. Elmstruck took the card and placed it in his wallet. His ego didn't want to, but his heart did. He gave me a hug and a kiss on my forehead. He looked at the table where his empty cup was. There was a crack at the bottom of it. He took his favorite cup, shaking his head in disbelief. He mumbled quietly as he walked out the door. I looked out the window. Mr. Elmstruck continued walking down the street with a mean face, holding the cup firmly in his bruised hands.

CPSIA information can be obtained
at www.ICGtesting.com
Printed in the USA
BVHW060833151222
654216BV00011B/861

9 781638 379454